CLEMENTINE ROSE
ROSE
and the Wedding Wobbles

Books by Jacqueline Harvey

Clementine Rose and the Surprise Visitor
Clementine Rose and the Pet Day Disaster
Clementine Rose and the Perfect Present
Clementine Rose and the Farm Fiasco
Clementine Rose and the Seaside Escape
Clementine Rose and the Treasure Box
Clementine Rose and the Famous Friend
Clementine Rose and the Ballet Break-In
Clementine Rose and the Movie Magic
Clementine Rose and the Birthday Emergency
Clementine Rose and the Special Promise
Clementine Rose and the Paris Puzzle

Alice-Miranda at School
Alice-Miranda on Holiday
Alice-Miranda Takes the Lead
Alice-Miranda at Sea
Alice-Miranda in New York
Alice-Miranda Shows the Way
Alice-Miranda in Paris
Alice-Miranda Shines Bright
Alice-Miranda in Japan
Alice-Miranda at Camp
Alice-Miranda at the Palace
Alice-Miranda in the Alps
Alice-Miranda to the Rescue
Alice-Miranda in China
Alice-Miranda Holds the Key

CLEMENTINE ROSE
and the Wedding Wobbles

Jacqueline Harvey

RANDOM HOUSE AUSTRALIA

A Random House book
Published by Penguin Random House Australia Pty Ltd
Level 3, 100 Pacific Highway, North Sydney NSW 2060
www.penguin.com.au

Penguin
Random House
Australia

First published by Random House Australia in 2017

Addresses for the Penguin Random House group of companies can be
found at global.penguinrandomhouse.com/offices.

National Library of Australia
Cataloguing-in-Publication entry

Author: Jacqueline Harvey
Title: Clementine Rose and the wedding wobbles/Jacqueline Harvey
ISBN: 978 0 85798 790 7 (pbk)
Series: Harvey, Jacqueline. Clementine Rose; 13
Target audience: For primary school age
Subjects: Weddings – Juvenile fiction
        Children's stories

Cover and internal illustrations by J.Yi
Cover design and additional illustration by Leanne Beattie
Internal design by Midland Typesetters, Australia
Typeset in ITC Century 12.5/19 by Midland Typesetters, Australia
Printed in Australia by Griffin Press, an accredited ISO AS/NZS
14001:2004 Environmental Management System printer

Penguin Random House Australia uses papers that are natural, renewable
and recyclable products and made from wood grown in sustainable forests.
The logging and manufacturing processes are expected to conform to the
environmental regulations of the country of origin.

For Ian and Olivia

PREMIERE

Clementine Rose adjusted the bow in her hair and smoothed the imaginary creases in her pretty white dress. It was her favourite of the costumes Mrs Mogg had made for her to wear in Basil Hobbs's new documentary. She turned to the teacup pig sitting on the floor beside her.

'What do you think, Lavender?' the girl asked.

The creature was wearing her best red collar and lead for the occasion. Lavender

1

looked up at her mistress and grunted her approval.

Clementine grinned, then an unpleasant thought happened upon her and she bit her lip. 'Do you think I'll sound silly up there on the screen? What if everyone laughs at me?'

Lady Clarissa Appleby poked her head around the door of the dressing room and smiled. 'I can't imagine it, sweetheart,' she said, walking in. 'You did a wonderful job during the filming, and I'm glad you're wearing that dress again. Margaret will be so pleased.'

'I love it,' Clementine said, swishing the skirt from side to side. 'Do you think Mrs Mogg has nearly finished my flower girl's dress?'

Clarissa nodded. 'We're going to pay her a visit tomorrow morning. You'll have to try it on so she can adjust the hem and see if any extra-special touches need to be added.'

'What do you mean?' Clementine asked. She couldn't picture the dress being any more perfect than it already was.

'Margaret's worried it might be a bit plain, but we'll see. I'm sure you'll know exactly what it needs. You have much more of an eye for fashion than I do – you and Aunt Violet are cut from the same cloth in that way,' Clarissa said. She picked up her daughter's hairbrush from the dressing table and popped it into her handbag. 'But I'm still going to make you wait to see my dress. I want you all to have a surprise.'

'I'm sure it's beautiful.' Clementine smiled. 'Mummy, don't you think it's funny how Aunt Violet and I both like clothes so much?' she mused. 'It must be because our eyes are exactly the same colour.'

'That must be it.' Clarissa knelt down to look into her daughter's bright blue eyes. 'Are you ready for your starring moment?'

Clementine shrugged. 'I think so.'

Finally, after many months of editing, Basil Hobbs's documentary on historic houses was set to premiere at the village hall in Penberthy Floss. Clementine had been tasked with the honour of introducing the film, in character as her great-grandmother.

Drew and Will appeared in the doorway, looking dapper in their suits, along with Aunt Violet. The sounds of murmuring and the scraping of chairs on the timber floor of the recently rebuilt hall filtered in from outside.

'Are there many people here?' Clementine asked in a wobbly voice.

'It looks like the whole village and half of Highton Mill has come to see you,' Will said excitedly.

Clementine felt her tummy flutter ever so slightly.

'How are you feeling?' Drew asked her. The corners of his eyes crinkled as he flashed a warm smile.

Clementine suddenly felt better. 'I was quite nervous at first,' she admitted, 'but then I had a long talk with Granny and Grandpa before we left. They said I should enjoy myself and think about how lucky I am to have such an amazing opportunity at my age.'

Will chuckled. 'Your grandparents are pretty smart, even if they are –' The boy stopped and looked up at his father, who had nudged him. Will's eyes darted down to the space between his shoes. 'Well, they *are*,' he whispered.

'I know it's only their portraits on the wall, but I still like to talk to them,' Clementine said plainly. 'They're always very encouraging, particularly when I need it the most. And they're good listeners too.'

Aunt Violet paused in the middle of re-applying her lipstick. 'I don't remember your grandfather uttering a rational word for at least a decade before he kicked the bucket,' she snorted. 'But if the old codger speaks sense to you, Clementine, then I'd say you have a better deal than the rest of us ever did.'

Clementine and Will looked at each other and giggled just as Basil arrived on the scene. He craned his neck through the impossibly crowded doorway to see if Clementine was ready. 'Why don't you all take your seats?' he suggested to the others. 'We're about to start. I can help Clemmie onto the stage from the wings.'

'Good luck,' Will said, giving her a hug.

Clarissa and Drew embraced the girl as well before Aunt Violet asked if she might have a moment alone with the child.

Clementine's stomach twisted. She had a sneaking suspicion it might have something to do with the perfume bottle she'd found in the bathroom. She had unscrewed the lid and put a few dabs on her wrist and neck the way Aunt Violet always did. Everything would have been all right if the woman's sphynx cat hadn't jumped up onto the sink and toppled the bottle over, causing its entire contents to dribble down the drain. Clementine had tried to tell her mother and Aunt Violet what had happened, but they'd been busy with guests. She'd forgotten all about it until now.

The old woman walked into the room and closed the door. 'Clementine –'

'It was my fault,' the child blurted, her eyes filling with tears.

Aunt Violet stopped and looked at her quizzically. 'What on earth are you talking about?' she asked.

Clementine's tears wobbled uncertainly. 'I didn't mean for your perfume to go down the sink,' she began slowly, then added, 'But it was really Pharaoh's fault.'

'I should have realised that bathroom smelt a lot better than it usually does,' Aunt Violet said with an amused curl to her lips. 'You needn't worry, Clementine. I wasn't overly fond of that scent anyway, and your mother found a bottle of my favourite in the cupboard this afternoon. She'd won a lovely gift pack months ago and was keeping it very quiet.'

'So, that's not why you wanted to talk to me?' Clementine brushed her eyes. She tried to remember what else she might have done recently to warrant a private audience with her great-aunt.

Violet Appleby shook her head. 'I wanted to say that I know we've had our moments, but . . . you do make me very proud.'

Clementine rubbed her ear, wondering if she'd heard correctly. As the old woman's face softened into a smile, Clementine's did too.

'Thank you, Aunt Violet,' she said, and hugged her around the middle. Clementine then stepped back to smooth her dress. 'I promise to do my best out there.'

'I know you will,' the old woman said with a wink.

As the credits rolled, the crowd burst into applause and some audience members even rose to their feet. Digby Pertwhistle was surprised to have learned a few things about the house he'd lived in for much of his life and made a mental note to locate the hidden cupboard in the library as soon as they got home. Clementine joined Basil onstage and offered them a curtsey.

'Did you enjoy making the movie, Clemmie?' Mr Tribble called out over the clapping.

Clementine grinned and nodded. 'It was fun most of the time, Mr Tribble, although there is an awful lot of sitting around and

doing things over and over again.' She cupped her hand to the side of her mouth as if she were telling a secret. 'Sometimes it was a bit boring,' she added with a giggle.

The audience laughed loudly.

Ethel Bottomley raised her hand. 'Would you like to become an actress when you're older?' she asked the girl.

Clementine swished her skirt as she considered the question. 'Maybe, but it would have to fit in with other things, like being a writer and a ballerina and a teacher and looking after animals and helping Mummy run the hotel,' she said. 'Oh, and being a flower girl for Mummy's wedding.'

'That's not a job,' Joshua Tribble heckled. 'And who would want to be a stupid flower girl anyway?'

Mrs Tribble glared at her son. 'I don't think you'd look very good in a dress, so I wouldn't worry about it if I were you.'

The boy's face turned bright red as a titter of laughter made its way around the hall.

Basil took the opportunity to step in and wind up the proceedings. 'Well, thank you all very much for your attendance this evening,' he said graciously. 'Please do stay and enjoy the delicious supper Mrs Mogg and her team have prepared.'

There was another hearty round of applause as Clementine and Basil walked offstage, where they were greeted by their families.

Digby Pertwhistle reached out to shake the man's hand. 'Bravo, Basil!' he exclaimed. 'The documentary is a smashing success and you've certainly done a great job making Penberthy House look very grand. I suspect our phone will be ringing off the hook after the film airs on television tonight.'

'That's all we need with the wedding coming up,' Aunt Violet muttered.

Clementine was surprised by her tone. She had thought that her great-aunt might have had something to say about her per-formance, but the woman seemed to have forgotten all about their earlier conversation. Clementine followed Aunt Violet's eyes and noticed an envelope poking out of the woman's handbag. It had a funny stamp on it that Clementine didn't recognise.

'Are you all right, Aunt Violet?' she asked.

'I'm fine,' the old woman sighed. 'Here, you'd better take Lavender for a walk outside. She probably needs a toilet stop.'

Violet Appleby passed Clementine the little pig's lead and snapped her bag shut.

THE LOST LETTER

Violet Appleby sat down on the end of her bed and reached into her handbag. She pulled out the envelope and turned it over in her hands, her fingers trembling as she picked at the seal. There were two pages. It seemed silly now to be afraid of such a flimsy thing. The first page was an official-looking document, its message short and blunt, like a savage blow from an angry fist.

> *Dear Miss Appleby,*
>
> *I regret to inform you that your daughter, Eliza Lindström, has passed away after a short illness. In the event of her death, she instructed that I pass on the enclosed letter.*
>
> *Yours sincerely,*
> *Piers Karlsson*
> Solicitor

Violet squeezed her eyes shut, summoning the strength to read the second letter. She knew she had to – she owed her daughter that much. So, with a deep breath, Violet forged on.

> *Dearest Mamma,*
>
> *I am sorry that fate has not allowed us to meet again. I still remember the day Pappa took me away. He told me you never wanted to hear from me again, but I suppose that in my heart*

I always knew it was a lie. Over the years, I wrote many letters to you and all of them went unanswered. It was only when Pappa passed away that I found them hidden, unopened, in a box – and the truth was finally revealed to me. I wonder, in all that time, did you try to find me?

Please do not succumb to anger or sadness; I have led a good and happy life. Do not punish yourself for our estrangement; life is often far more complicated than we wish. If in time you find your way back to your family, I hope you will visit my cousin, Clarissa. She is like a sister to me, with the kindest of hearts. Perhaps you will find some comfort and unexpected joy with her, as I always did.

Your loving daughter,
Eliza

Violet reread the letter at least a dozen times. Through a haze of tears, she eventually noticed the date in the top right-hand corner and gasped. If the letter had been written over six years ago, why had she only just received it? Violet resolved to telephone the solicitor first thing on Monday morning to make sense of the timelines.

But the one fact remained. The ache that Violet often felt in her heart was now one hundred times bigger than it had ever been before. That night she cried herself to sleep and dreamt of a precious little girl who was lost to her forever.

A CURIOUS GUEST

larissa Appleby waltzed from one side of the kitchen to the other, counting her steps as she twirled. She had hoped to fit in a few practice sessions with her fiancé, Drew, but he was busy with a project he had to finish before the wedding.

'One-two-three, one-two-three,' Clarissa sang as her feet followed suit. She picked up two rashers of bacon and tossed them into the sizzling pan, then glided to the toaster, delivering two slices of bread into the slots.

'Good morning, dear. You're up early,' Digby Pertwhistle said as he fetched his apron from the butler's pantry.

Clarissa spun around, her cheeks aflame. 'Oh dear, you've caught me again.'

'I don't know what you're talking about,' the old man said with a smile. He pointed to the pan. 'We didn't have anyone staying last night, did we?'

'I thought I'd take breakfast up to Aunt Violet,' Clarissa said as she added a ripe-red tomato cut into halves, then cracked two large eggs into the fry-up.

Digby raised an eyebrow. 'What's happened now?'

'I'm not sure,' Clarissa said, a faint crease appearing across the top of her nose. 'I passed Aunt Violet's room last night and she sounded upset. When I called out to ask her if there was anything I could do, she told me in no uncertain terms to mind my own business. I hope it's nothing serious.'

Digby put his hand on Clarissa's shoulder. 'It might have something to do with that letter I signed for a few days ago,' he said in hushed tones. 'You know it was from Sweden.'

'I had wondered,' Clarissa replied, biting her lip.

Their conversation was interrupted by the sound of Clementine thudding down the back stairs with Lavender skittering after her. 'I'm starving and that bacon smells delicious,' the girl announced. 'No offence, Lavender.'

The little pig didn't seem to mind in the least and ran off to find Pharaoh, who was doing yoga stretches in front of the range.

Clarissa turned and smiled at her daughter. 'Would you like bacon and eggs? Or I could make some pancakes after I take this up to Aunt Violet.'

The door from the hallway swung open. 'No need to take anything up for me,' Aunt Violet said, marching into the room. 'I'll have toast, as per usual.'

Clarissa and Digby exchanged curious looks.

'How are you feeling, Aunt Violet?' Clarissa asked.

'Tiptop,' the woman said, plonking herself down beside Clementine. She was dressed in a smart pair of cream trousers and a lovely red silk blouse.

'Oh!' Clementine gasped, startling the woman. 'I almost forgot.'

She dashed over to the noticeboard, where her mother pinned school notes and important reminders. Clementine picked up a thick black pen, then climbed onto a stool and put a big cross on the special calendar she'd made to count down the days until the wedding.

'Mummy, there are only six more days to go!' she exclaimed.

'Don't remind me, Clementine,' Uncle Digby said with a shudder. 'I've still got a speech to write and I don't know when I'll ever get time to practise.'

'Granny and Grandpa are good listeners,' Clementine reminded him. She jumped to the ground. 'I've been reciting my wedding poem to them every day.'

She thought Aunt Violet would probably have something to say about that, but the woman didn't utter a word.

'If you don't want your bacon and eggs, Aunt Violet, I'll have them,' Clementine said, scampering back to the table. 'I must have been a lot more nervous than I thought last night because I didn't really eat anything. I could eat a horse now.'

'Well, I hope not,' Aunt Violet said, glancing in the child's direction. She paused, her eyes widening. 'I know someone else who used to say that when she was little . . .'

The woman's voice trailed off as she gazed, dumbstruck, at Clementine.

Clementine peered back at her. She'd once heard Mrs Bottomley telling a classmate's mother about her next-door neighbour who had a stroke right in front of her. Apparently, the woman had been talking when all of a sudden she stopped mid-sentence and started staring into space.

Clementine waved a hand in front of Aunt Violet's face. 'Mummy, come quickly,' she called.

Violet Appleby's eyes brimmed with tears, making her irises an even more brilliant blue than usual.

Clarissa and Digby both raced over to see what the matter was.

'Aunt Violet, are you all right?' Clarissa asked. She snapped her fingers and offered the woman a tissue from her apron pocket.

Violet continued to stare at Clementine as if she were gazing upon the most precious object in the world. She took the tissue and dabbed at her eyes. 'Of course I'm all right,' she whispered.

'I think Aunt Violet needs a cup of tea, Uncle Digby,' Clementine said. She slipped out of her chair and stood beside the old woman.

Violet Appleby wrapped her arms around the child and squeezed her like a python. Clementine squirmed to get free.

The odd scene was interrupted by the telephone ringing.

Clarissa hurried over to answer it while Digby filled the teapot with boiling water. Seconds later, he placed a cup of tea in front of Aunt Violet and followed it up with two pieces of buttery toast.

After Clarissa took a booking for two couples, the telephone didn't stop ringing for the next half-hour. It turned out that quite a few people had watched Basil's documentary and were dying to visit Penberthy House in person. Digby Pertwhistle set about preparing everyone's breakfast, but Clarissa was up and down like a yo-yo, sipping her tepid tea between calls.

'Godfathers! How are you to prepare for the wedding *and* look after all those guests at the same time, Clarissa?' Violet tutted.

Clementine surmised that the woman must be feeling better. Aunt Violet was starting to sound a lot more like herself.

'We'll manage,' Clarissa said, finally sitting long enough to nibble on a piece of toast.

'Besides, we're closing for two weeks while we're away on our honeymoon. I wouldn't expect you and Uncle Digby to manage everything on your own.'

'Where exactly are we going, Mummy?' Clementine asked.

Aunt Violet scoffed. 'Don't be ridiculous, Clementine. You won't be going anywhere.'

'But Mummy and Drew said that it was a familymoon,' Clementine protested.

Aunt Violet pursed her lips. 'What a preposterous idea! Your mother and Drew need some grown-up time. Pertwhistle and I can look after you and Will.'

'But I thought we were going somewhere at the seaside,' Clementine said. She was beginning to feel quite hot and bothered.

'Over my dead body,' Aunt Violet said. 'It's far too dangerous. Need I mention what happened last time, when you and Freddy almost perished in that cave?'

'Perhaps we should discuss it later, when

everyone has had more time to think about it,' Clarissa said, eager to avoid an argument.

'But me and Will want to go and it's the holidays,' Clementine said, a tad louder than she had intended.

'Will and *I*,' Aunt Violet corrected. 'One of these days, Clementine, you will learn to speak the Queen's English and, no, I forbid it.'

Clementine stamped her foot. 'You can't tell Mummy and Drew what to do!'

'Clemmie!' Clarissa said sternly, then immediately softened her tone. 'Why don't you take Lavender outside to play in the garden? We'll see Mrs Mogg about your dress in a little while.'

The front doorbell rang.

'I'll get it,' Digby offered. He smiled tensely at Clarissa before hurrying out into the hallway.

'You'll need to be careful of the bees in the back garden, Clementine,' Aunt Violet said. 'There must be a hive somewhere close by.

I saw thousands of them yesterday and I'd bet my house on you being allergic.'

Clementine ignored her great-aunt and slid off her chair. She stomped over to where Lavender was lying beside Pharaoh in their basket. 'Come on, Lavender, I need some fresh air. It's very stuffy in here.'

She picked up the little pig and walked outside just as Digby poked his head around the door.

'Excuse me,' he said, 'am I right in thinking that the Sage Room is free this evening?'

Clarissa hopped up to consult the register. 'Yes. We've got a couple in the Rose Room, but the Sage Room is available.'

'Are you happy for me to take the booking?' Digby asked. 'I'll run up and make sure the room hasn't befallen any strange happenings overnight before I show Mr Johansson upstairs. I'll have him wait in the sitting room in the meantime.'

Clarissa nodded. 'Of course.'

Digby Pertwhistle scurried away, leaving

Clarissa pondering whether she might have bitten off a little more than she could chew.

Outside, Clementine and Lavender had wandered around to the front of the house. Clementine had decided the fastest way to get over her stoush with Aunt Violet was to make up a poem, which she was now reciting loudly on the porch while Lavender snuffled about in the garden.

'There once was a meanie called Vi, who swallowed a big fat fly. It tumbled and turned and rumbled and churned till she spat it back out in the sky,' Clementine said, raising her arm dramatically into the air. She thought for a second, then added, 'And she got a big fat tummy ache, which she totally deserved.'

Clementine was startled to hear someone clapping.

'That was very good,' said a voice filled with laughter.

Clementine turned to find a man standing there. He was tall and slim with a head of thick blond hair. 'Hello,' she said with an embarrassed smile. 'I didn't really mean it about Aunt Violet getting a tummy ache.'

'I won't tell her if you don't,' the man promised with a wink.

Clementine grinned. She liked the way the man's blue eyes twinkled. 'Are you staying here?' she asked.

'Yes, I hope so,' the man replied. He sat down on the top step and looked at the child. 'You don't happen to know Clementine Rose, the girl who was delivered in a basket of dinner rolls, do you?'

Clementine laughed. 'That's me! I know it's not how most children find their mothers, but I think it was the best way for me. Anyway, I'd better go. Mummy's getting married and we have to see Mrs Mogg about my dress.'

'Married?' the man said in surprise.

Clementine nodded. 'To Drew. And I'm getting a brother called Will.'

'It's very special to have a brother, but how do you feel about that?' the man asked.

'I can't wait. I love them both,' Clementine said. 'Bye!'

She waved and darted back in through the front door, where she almost bumped into Uncle Digby.

'Ooh, careful, Clementine,' the old butler said. 'By the way, did you see a fellow out there? It seems our new guest has gone walkabout.'

'Yes, he's a very nice man and he's on the porch,' Clementine called as she dashed down the hall with Lavender tripping along behind her. 'He asked me about the dinner rolls.'

Digby Pertwhistle spun around. 'Why ever would he do that?' he wondered aloud, then went off in search of his missing guest.

FULL HOUSE

Clementine poked her head around the kitchen door, wary that Aunt Violet may have lingered after breakfast. She let out a little sigh of relief when she saw her mother standing alone at the sink, up to her elbows in soap suds.

Clementine skipped into the room with Lavender beside her. 'Hello Mummy. What time are we seeing Mrs Mogg?' she asked.

Clarissa looked up from her task and glanced at the clock above the door. 'Oh dear, we're due there in twenty minutes.'

There was a shuffling sound and Aunt Violet emerged from the butler's pantry, loaded up with what looked to be the ingredients of a cake.

Clementine recoiled at the thought of her great-aunt baking, then considered asking the woman to let her lick the beaters.

The telephone rang for the umpteenth time that morning.

'I'll get it,' Clementine sang, and hurried over to answer it.

Aunt Violet rolled her eyes. 'Good heavens, when is it going to stop?'

Clementine used her best telephone voice and asked if the person would mind holding for a moment. She put her hand over the mouthpiece and informed her mother that it was someone who wanted to make a booking for that night.

Clarissa peeled off her rubber gloves and took the phone. After what felt like an eternity, she finally hung up. 'That's it,' she declared, collapsing into a chair. 'It's a full house this evening and every single person wants to have dinner. I hadn't realised that Basil's film would have such an instantaneous effect. I'm going to have to put off visiting Margaret until tomorrow afternoon.'

Clementine's shoulders drooped.

'I'll take Clemmie to see her,' Aunt Violet volunteered as she finished sifting the flour, sugar and cocoa powder for the cake into the giant mixing bowl.

Clementine blanched.

'Are you sure?' Clarissa asked.

'Absolutely,' Aunt Violet said. 'Let's face it, Clarissa, I'll know immediately if the dress is right or not. I have a far better idea of what suits the child.'

'I know what suits me,' Clementine said crossly.

'Of course you do. You're ...' Aunt Violet hesitated. 'An Appleby.'

Clementine eyed the ingredients on the bench. 'What about your cake?'

The old woman dusted her hands and set about fixing herself a quick cup of tea. 'I'll pick up where I left off this afternoon, or Pertwhistle can make it. He seems to like whipping things up.'

'What am I whipping now?' the man said, sweeping into the room with a basket of dirty laundry and a cheeky grin on his face.

Aunt Violet flushed and glared at him.

'Uncle Digby, I'm afraid you won't have time to do any washing today. We've got a full house as of a few minutes ago,' Clarissa informed him.

Digby frowned and put down the hamper. 'I thought we were full on the last call I took.'

Clarissa rushed over to consult the reservations book. 'Heavens,' she gasped. 'I've double-booked the Rose Room! My head is a complete muddle.'

'That's because you've got too much to think about,' Aunt Violet scolded. 'The wedding is just around the corner, Clarissa. What were you thinking taking in all those guests tonight? I hope you've struck a line through next week.'

Clarissa seemed to wilt on the spot. 'I suppose I was caught up in everyone else's excitement about the house,' she sighed. 'We've never had so many enquiries at once before. What a pity Basil didn't make the documentary years ago. We'd have been able to renovate from top to bottom by now.'

'Don't you worry, Clarissa. We'll manage,' Uncle Digby said. He gave her shoulder a reassuring squeeze. 'Would you like me to call the last people and let them know we've made a mistake?'

Clarissa shook her head. 'You don't have to do it. I'll apologise profusely and offer them a discount if they reschedule. Perhaps there might be a room at the Rose and Donkey. They've started offering accommodation again recently.'

'Hello, hello, where's my favourite bride-to-be?' a shrill voice echoed through the hall.

Sebastian Smote's face appeared around the door, soon followed by the rest of his nattily dressed figure.

Clementine brightened at the sight of the man. 'I love your tie, Mr Smote,' she said with a wave.

'Godfathers, what's next? Dive-bombing penguins?' Aunt Violet mumbled.

'Oh, Miss Appleby, you know me too well.' The man laughed heartily. 'I have the sweetest white tie with the tiny black-and-white birds all over, but it doesn't go with this gorgeous green jacket. It was flying pigs today – there was simply no other choice.'

Aunt Violet rolled her eyes and buried her face in the recipe book, pretending to see what she needed to put into the cake mix next.

Sebastian Smote, wedding planner extraordinaire, was one of the most fabulous people Clementine knew. He had become a frequent visitor to Penberthy House over the past year or so, since they had started hosting weddings. When he found out that Clarissa and Drew

were getting married, he'd insisted on helping with the planning free of charge. The only trouble was, Sebastian Smote and Aunt Violet didn't often see eye to eye.

'Look, Mr Smote, I've been practising my walk,' Clementine said. She took three very slow and deliberate steps, then stopped and pretended to scatter rose petals before taking another three measured paces.

'You'll have to speed it up, Clementine, or we'll be waiting an hour for you to get down the aisle,' Aunt Violet said.

'No, no, no, that's absolutely splendid,' Sebastian insisted. 'Your aunt doesn't know anywhere near as much about weddings as I do,' he whispered loudly.

'Don't you believe it,' the old woman muttered under her breath.

Uncle Digby stuffed his fist into his mouth to stop himself from laughing, but Clarissa was feeling a little overwhelmed by her visitor. She took a deep breath and tried to keep her composure. 'I hadn't realised that you were coming this morning, Mr Smote.'

'Oh, my dear, there is plenty to do. First up, we need to confirm the flowers and the music. I've got some lanterns outside I want to show you and there's the aviary, which I'm going to fill with doves on the back lawn, and a cherub fountain for the front garden.' The man grinned.

Violet Appleby's lips quivered. 'I'm sorry, Clarissa, but I simply must intervene. We can have flowers and music, but we are *not* having any of that other nonsense. Clarissa's wedding,' she said, turning to Mr Smote, 'is to be a *classy* affair.'

Sebastian batted his hand at the woman. 'But *of course*. My weddings are nothing but class, Miss Appleby. There's no need to worry about that. There's just so much to do and so little time, but I could murder a cup of tea first, and you must tell me who that handsome fellow was I passed in the hallway.'

'I imagine that was Mr Johansson,' Uncle Digby said, fetching the kettle.

'He was the man with the sparkly eyes I met outside before,' Clementine added. 'He made me laugh and he asked me if it was true I came in a basket of dinner rolls.'

The butler's forehead wrinkled in surprise. 'Ah, I didn't realise that's what you meant earlier, Clemmie. How curious that he asked you about that.'

'Well, it's none of his business,' Aunt Violet huffed.

'He seems a nice enough chap,' Uncle Digby said. 'He told me he stayed at the pub last night and was looking for more comfortable accommodation.'

'Oh, that sounds ominous,' Clarissa said. 'Perhaps I shouldn't mention the Rose and Donkey to the double-booked guests.'

'Why don't you offer them my room and Clementine and I can bunk in together?' Aunt Violet suggested.

Clementine almost choked on the glass of milk she'd just poured for herself.

Digby and Clarissa looked at each other.

'No, of course we won't have you do that,' Clarissa said, wondering at her aunt's sudden generosity.

'I'd prefer you keep the guests happy and, besides, Clementine and I will make cosy room mates,' Aunt Violet said.

Clementine wasn't so sure about that. The woman snored even louder than Uncle Digby and sometimes she talked in her sleep too.

'If you're certain,' Clarissa said, sounding far from convinced herself.

Aunt Violet nodded. 'Pertwhistle can move some of my things while I take Clementine to see Margaret. Could you call her, Clarissa, and say we're running late?'

Clementine was confused, and she wasn't the only one. It wasn't like Aunt Violet to be so helpful.

Mr Smote whipped out his notebook. 'Now that's sorted, shall we make some decisions? Roses and peonies, or irises and violets? What's it to be, Clarissa?'

TROUBLE

'How come we're walking?' Clementine asked as she and Aunt Violet set off across the field to the village. Aunt Violet hardly ever walked anywhere.

'It's safer,' the woman replied.

Clementine nodded. 'Everyone says you drive too fast.'

'I beg your pardon. There is nothing wrong with my driving, thank you very much,' Aunt Violet sniffed. 'It's all those other maniacs on the road one simply can't trust.'

The pair emerged by the rectory, where Father Bob was busy trimming the roses in his front garden. He waved and walked over to the low stone wall. 'Congratulations on last night, little one,' he said, handing Clementine a beautiful pink bloom.

But before she could accept it, Aunt Violet snatched it from the man's hand. 'What were you thinking, Father?' the woman said, waving the flower in his face. 'There are thorns on this stem. Clementine could have cut her finger or worse!'

She handed the offending bloom back to him as Clementine watched on in dismay.

'I – I didn't realise,' the man stammered, trying to see where he'd missed a barb.

'Next time you give someone a rose, you need to ensure it isn't a deadly weapon,' Aunt Violet tutted, shaking her head.

Adrian, the minister's dribbly bulldog, was sitting under the pear tree nearby. He suddenly expelled a thunderous gust of wind, which shrouded the trio in an eye-watering stench. Clementine held her nose and burst out laughing. Father Bob, although sheepish at first, did too.

'Good heavens, Father!' Violet sputtered. 'Perhaps you should lay off the ginger beer. With gas like that, you could set fire to the entire village.'

The man's face reddened. 'You don't think that was me, do you, Miss Appleby?'

'Well, I can't imagine Clementine is capable of producing such an evil concoction and there doesn't seem to be any sign of your dog,' the woman said.

Sure enough, Adrian had scampered away at exactly the wrong moment.

Aunt Violet took hold of the girl's hand. 'Excuse us, Father. We'd better go and see Mrs Mogg or she'll think we're not coming.'

The child waved goodbye to Father Bob with her free hand as her great-aunt led her to the kerb. The woman looked left and right, then left again. Seeing that the roadway was

clear, Clementine stepped off the kerb only
to feel herself jerked backwards.

'Stop right there, young lady,' Aunt Violet
demanded.

Clementine peered in either direction
but couldn't see a single thing. The road was
empty apart from a car already parked outside
the shop. They stood there a minute longer
while Aunt Violet watched and waited. She
looked left, right and left again at least three
more times.

Clementine began to sway on the spot.
'Aunt Violet, the road is clear,' she said
impatiently.

'Oh, very well, Clementine,' the old woman
replied testily. 'Stop your whining.'

Violet Appleby promptly scooped up the
girl and rushed her across the road, depositing
her neatly in front of the shop with the
tinkly bell.

Margaret Mogg's sewing room had been converted from a spare bedroom. It had racks full of fabric along one wall, a huge table for cutting patterns in the centre and a sewing machine and an overlocker too. Clementine hoped Mrs Mogg would give her sewing lessons when she was older.

The baby-blue dress fit like a glove and Clementine loved it from the moment she looked in the long mirror. But Mrs Mogg was right. It was a little plain for a flower girl's dress. The woman tried bows and appliqués and all manner of other adornments before Clementine suggested flowers. And it turned out that Mrs Mogg had just the thing.

'What about something like this?' she asked, pulling out two pink flowers made from the finest silk thread. 'It won't take long to make some more.'

Aunt Violet nodded her approval. 'Yes. Scattered across the bodice and skirt with a concentration around the waist.'

'They're perfect,' Clementine gushed, clasping her hands together. 'I'll be a proper flower girl now. I can't wait to tell Mummy.'

'Why don't you leave it as a surprise?' Aunt Violet suggested.

'Do you think Mummy would like that?' Clementine frowned. She really wanted to tell her mother as soon as they got home.

'I'm sure she would,' Aunt Violet said. 'In fact, your dress has confirmed precisely what type of flowers we need for the marquee. I'll call the florist and change them first thing in the morning.'

'But Mr Smote was checking the flowers with Mummy,' Clementine said.

Aunt Violet couldn't help the look of contempt that flashed across her face. 'Sebastian Smote has done quite enough. *I'll* be taking over from now on,' she harrumphed. 'We don't need him mincing about the house with his preposterous ideas. I don't know why your mother puts up with him.'

Clementine looked at Mrs Mogg and the pair exchanged a wry smile.

Aunt Violet craned her neck, glancing around Mrs Mogg's workroom. 'I forgot to mention that Clarissa asked if I might take a peek at her dress to make sure it was all right,' she said.

Clementine looked at the woman. 'But I thought Mummy wants it to be a surprise for everyone?'

Margaret Mogg tsked and shook her head. 'I'm afraid Clementine's right. I'm under strict instructions not to show anyone.'

'What a lot of fuss and bother.' Aunt Violet wrinkled her lip and stood up to gather her things. 'Come along, Clementine. We'd best be getting back. I have a million things to do and no doubt your mother and Pertwhistle will be completely snowed under with a house full of guests. Honestly, the place is crowded enough already and it is only going to get more so.'

'Oh, there is something else.' Mrs Mogg bustled over to her sewing table and picked up a length of pink fabric. 'I've made a ribbon for Lavender. She is going to the wedding, I assume.'

Clementine beamed. 'She wouldn't miss it. Thank you, Mrs Mogg.'

'And would you mind taking the cushion? Will might like to practise carrying it for his ring-bearing duties,' Margaret Mogg said. She handed Clementine a small bag containing the pretty white pillow.

Clementine gave Mrs Mogg a hug and followed Aunt Violet out of the shop. Claws, the Moggs' tabby cat, was lounging by the front door. Clementine bent down and gave him a rub on his tummy.

'Be careful of that cat, Clemmie,' Aunt Violet warned. 'He is a vicious beast.'

Clementine looked at the sleepy puss. She had no idea what Aunt Violet was talking about. Claws was just about the laziest creature she had ever met.

A SNOOP

Clementine spotted Will playing in the garden with Lavender as she and Aunt Violet neared the house. Bubbling with excitement, the girl ran ahead and through the rusty gate to tell him all about her dress fitting. She then handed over the ring cushion and explained what it was for to the bewildered boy. They decided to practise walking down the aisle later, but with fake rings, of course. They didn't want to lose the real ones in the grass.

'Hello darling,' Lady Clarissa called from the back door. 'How did you go with Margaret?'

'I love my dress! I'd wear it every day if you'd let me,' Clementine fizzed. 'We added something to it that's extra special, but Aunt Violet says it's a surprise. She also tried to trick Mrs Mogg into showing us your dress, but she was a closed ship.'

Violet Appleby rolled her eyes at the child. 'I think you'll find that's a closed shop, Clementine.'

'Aren't you the cheeky one, Aunt Violet?' Clarissa said, laughing. 'You know I'm keeping it under wraps.'

'I just wanted to make sure you aren't going to look like some country bumpkin or worse,' Violet replied. 'Speaking of country bumpkins, has Pertwhistle made that cake yet?'

Clarissa shook her head. 'Poor Uncle Digby has been rushed off his feet. We're actually not looking too bad, though, considering how many guests are booked in for tonight.'

Aunt Violet glanced around to make sure Sebastian Smote wasn't lurking about in the garden before she revealed her plans. 'Now, Clarissa,' she began, 'I'm rethinking the flowers and I've decided to tweak the seating arrangements. It's one of the riskiest things at any wedding. There's always a second cousin thrice removed who can't stand to be within reach of some other relative or there's likely to be blood.'

'You must have had lots of experience with that,' Clementine said seriously. She often heard Uncle Digby joke about how many husbands Aunt Violet had gone through.

The old woman tilted her chin upwards. 'I have planned a few weddings in my time,' she admitted, 'but not just my own, Miss Smartypants.'

After deciding that a picnic was in order, Clementine grabbed Will's hand and the pair raced off inside in search of supplies. They sprinted up the back stairs to the top floor of the house, where the family's bedrooms were located. Clementine pushed open the small door that led to the attic and hurried up the stairs while Will lagged behind.

'Oh, hello,' the boy heard Clementine say. 'Are you lost?'

Will reached the top and was surprised to see a man standing there. He had blond hair and wore dark-rimmed glasses.

'I'm sorry,' the man said. He returned a photograph to an old wooden box and quickly closed the lid. 'I took a wrong turn and ended up here. Then, I must admit, my curiosity got the better of me.'

'There is lots to look at,' Clementine agreed, 'but Theodore's my favourite.' She pointed to the stuffed warthog that stood in one corner of the room. 'We had a big clean-out a while ago and sold a load of things to raise money for the new village hall. Mummy says it's a waste having stuff hidden away when other people could get some use out of them. But we couldn't sell Theodore. He's family.'

'Theodore, you say?' The man grinned. 'He's very handsome . . . for a warthog.'

Clementine suddenly remembered her manners. 'This is Will,' she said, beckoning the boy forward. 'He's going to be my brother.'

Will took a few cautious steps into the room and waved.

'Hello there, it's nice to finally meet you,' said Mr Johansson.

'Where are you from?' Will asked, finding his voice.

'Sweden,' the man said. 'I suppose you think my accent is strange.'

'It's very cold there,' Will said. 'My dad was making a film in Stockholm and I got to go with him.'

'I hope you enjoyed it.' The fellow smiled. 'Well, I should be heading back downstairs.'

'Would you like to have a picnic with us?' Clementine asked.

'I think I had better do some work, actually,' Mr Johansson replied. 'And then perhaps I will go for a walk to the village. It seems a quaint place.'

'Yes, it's beautiful and Mrs Mogg sells really yummy lollies and cakes in her shop,' Clementine said.

'Do you like living here?' he asked, his blue eyes twinkling.

Clementine nodded. 'Penberthy House is the loveliest place to live in the whole world, especially now that the roof doesn't leak.'

'And your mother – is she kind?'

Clementine nodded again. 'Very. She's the best cook too and everyone loves her. Well, maybe not Aunt Violet when she first came to stay, but she's much nicer to Mummy now.'

'I am glad it worked out in the end. Well, enjoy your picnic and I hope to see you later.' The man smiled and left the children to it.

'Don't you think it was a bit weird that he was up here?' Will whispered, once the man had disappeared downstairs.

Clementine shrugged. 'I think he was just lost. It is a big house, after all,' she reasoned as she opened a cupboard door and pulled out a blanket and some cushions. 'Which bedroom are you going to have after the wedding?' she asked.

Will looked over at her. 'What do you mean?'

'Well, you have to pick a bedroom because Mummy and Drew will share,' Clementine said. 'Isn't that what married people do?'

Will gulped. It hadn't occurred to him that he and his father would have to move. 'But my room has stars on the ceiling,' he said.

Clementine stopped and thought for a second. 'I've got an idea. Aunt Violet should move into Crabtree Cottage and you can have the Blue Room. We can paint the ceiling so it's exactly the same as the one you have now. I'm sure Aunt Violet would rather live there than here with us. She hates the bathroom, and Crabtree Cottage has two brand-new ones.'

Will's brow furrowed. 'But why can't you come and live at Crabtree Cottage with us?' he asked.

'Because Mummy has to run the hotel,' Clementine replied. 'She can't be rushing back here from the village every time a guest needs something.'

'Uncle Digby and Aunt Violet could look after them,' Will said.

Clementine's neck felt hot and prickly. 'No, it's Mummy's hotel and she's in charge.' She picked up the blanket and hurled it over the balustrade and down the stairs, then catapulted the cushions after it.

A loud shriek sounded from below. Clementine and Will looked at each other, their eyes widening. Then they both ran down and leaned over the railing. At the bottom of the stairs, a blanket-clad ghost was wriggling about, trying to get free.

Clementine's hands flew to her mouth. 'Oh no!'

'Who's that?' Will asked.

'It's me!' the ghost barked as it wrestled the blanket off its head.

Clementine winced. 'Sorry, Aunt Violet.'

The old woman strode up the stairs. 'What are you two doing up here? Causing mischief, I gather.'

'We're going to have a picnic on the back lawn,' Clementine explained. 'What are you doing up here? I thought you hated the attic.'

'I remembered we once had a lot of lovely old cut-glass vases that we might be able to use for the flowers at the reception,' Aunt Violet replied. 'Unless, of course, your mother sold them at the fete.' Violet Appleby noticed the box on the table. 'Why did you have that out?'

Clementine looked at the box. 'We didn't.'

'It was that man who was up here,' Will said. 'He had it open.'

'Which man?' Aunt Violet demanded. 'Guests aren't supposed to be in the attic.'

'The nice man from Sweden who asked me about the dinner rolls,' Clementine said.

Violet Appleby's heart began to pound. *Sweden.* Pertwhistle hadn't mentioned their guest was from Sweden. What was he doing nosing around?

'Are you all right, Aunt Violet?' Clementine asked.

The woman shook herself and stood up straight. 'I don't like the idea of guests rummaging through our belongings,' she said, walking over to the row of old wardrobes. She began opening and closing doors in search of the vases.

'That's what I said,' Will agreed. 'But Clemmie thought he was lost.'

'Lost, my eye.' The woman turned and looked at the children with her hands on her hips. 'The man was snooping and I, for one, don't like snoops.'

Clementine thought that was a very funny thing for Aunt Violet to say. When the woman had first arrived at the house, she'd spent all her time sneaking about looking for Granny's jewels. As far as Clementine was concerned, Aunt Violet had proven to be the biggest snoop of all.

A QUIET WORD

Clementine was dressed and ready for school earlier than usual on Monday morning. She'd had a very bad dream and had woken up thinking about it. To make matters worse, Aunt Violet snored like a tractor. Even Lavender had retreated downstairs to sleep in Pharaoh's basket.

Clementine and Will's picnic the day before had been disappointing, to say the least. They had tried to practise their wedding march, but Will had kept walking too fast, and the lollies she'd tied to the cushion fell off and Lavender ate them, which is exactly what Clementine had warned would happen. Then Will got stroppy and said he didn't want to practise anymore. When Clementine asked him what the matter was, he refused to say a word and wandered around the garden in a sulk. The only bright note was that she had spent the rest of the afternoon collecting lady beetles, which seemed to have invaded the garden in their thousands.

Clementine hoped things would be better between her and Will this morning. She packed her schoolbag and walked down the back stairs as the clock in the entrance hall struck seven.

Her mother was lifting two boiled eggs out of a saucepan and into egg cups. Clarissa turned and smiled at her daughter. 'Hello darling, you're up early.'

Clementine nodded. 'I had a bad dream and Aunt Violet is snoring so loudly even Granny and Grandpa can hear her.'

'That's no good, but it's a new day and the sun is shining,' Clarissa said cheerfully.

Clementine wrinkled her nose. 'Mummy, what's that smell?'

'It's caviar paste.' Clarissa gestured to the pink worms she'd squeezed onto a small dish. 'It's a sandwich spread made from fish eggs.'

'I hope that's not my breakfast,' Clementine said as she marked off another day on the calendar. Unlike every other time she had done so, Clementine didn't feel nearly as excited. She walked back to the table and poured herself a glass of milk. 'Where's Uncle Digby?' she asked, just as the man walked through the swinging door.

'Good morning, Clemmie. How are you today?' he asked.

'I'm fine,' Clementine said a little glumly. She had her elbows on the table and was resting her head in her hands.

'It doesn't sound like it,' the man said. He handed Clarissa a piece of paper from the top of his notepad. 'Two fried eggs and bacon for

Mrs Swizzle and a serve of nut porridge for her husband. They've dashed upstairs to pack as they've got to catch an early train, but they'll be back down in ten minutes. I'll take that to Mr Johansson now.'

Clarissa quickly removed her apron and hung it up on the hook beside the stove. 'I'll take it. I'd like to have a quiet word while he's still on his own.'

'He's very nice,' Clementine said, drawing invisible pictures on her glass of milk with her finger. 'I don't think Aunt Violet likes him, though. She got very cross when she found out he'd been in the attic yesterday.'

Clarissa blinked. She hadn't a clue why the man would be pottering around their attic, of all places. She suspected he wasn't actually on holiday. Determined to get to the bottom of the matter, she picked up the plates and headed to the dining room, where their mysterious guest was flicking through the newspaper.

'Good morning, Mr Johansson.' Clarissa smiled at the man, who looked up and smiled back. 'How are you enjoying your stay?'

'Oh, I am having a marvellous time,' he replied warmly, taking off his spectacles. He set aside his newspaper and placed his napkin on his lap.

'Are you here for long?' Clarissa asked, setting his breakfast down in front of him.

'I'm not sure. Perhaps I will stay a while,' he said. 'As long as you have the room.'

The man spread some of the fish paste onto a slice of bread and cut it in half. Then he knocked the tops off his soft-boiled eggs and waved his knife in the air as if he were conducting an orchestra.

'I was wondering something about your daughter, Clementine,' he said. 'She is a most delightful child, although she was quite upset with her great-aunt yesterday morning. Does that happen a lot?'

Clarissa gulped, caught off-guard by such a curious question. 'I can assure you Aunt Violet adores Clemmie and the feeling is completely mutual. Clemmie was just annoyed about something silly. Nothing to worry about at –'

A bloodcurdling shriek sounded from the hallway.

'Clementine!' Aunt Violet thundered, her voice reverberating around the walls. 'There are bugs in my hair!'

Clarissa cringed. She excused herself and raced out of the room to find Aunt Violet at the top of the stairs. She was in her dressing-gown and slippers, and clawing at her silver mop.

'Aunt Violet, please calm down,' Clarissa whispered loudly. 'We have guests.'

Clementine barrelled through the kitchen door with Uncle Digby hot on her heels. The old butler wouldn't have missed this sight for all the world.

'My lady beetles!' Clementine exclaimed. 'I must have forgotten to put the lid back on the bug-catcher. There were so many in the garden yesterday and they were so pretty . . .' She looked up at Aunt Violet, who was less than impressed. 'They're supposed to be good luck too,' she said. Although they didn't seem to be good luck for her right at the moment.

Intrigued by the ruckus, Mr Johansson had emerged from the dining room and was peering up the staircase. Clarissa hurried back down, encouraging her guest to return to his breakfast with the promise of fresh coffee and pastries.

Stefan Johansson smiled to himself. There was now no doubt in his mind that he had found the right child and what he intended to do was absolutely the best thing for everyone.

MIXES AND MUDDLES

Clementine stared out of the window at the cows grazing in the field. It was nice to see them properly for a change, instead of them being one big blur.

'I'm sorry about the lady beetles,' she apologised for the tenth time, glancing at her great-aunt's face in the rear-vision mirror.

Violet Appleby raised her perfectly plucked left eyebrow while a wry smile perched on her lips. 'I suppose I should be thankful you weren't collecting worms or cockroaches.'

Clementine grinned and was about to confess that she'd like to catch cockroaches if only they didn't run so fast when she was distracted by a chorus of blasting car horns. The child wriggled around to investigate. Her eyes almost popped out of her head when she saw the long line of cars trailing behind them. The drivers looked very angry.

'I think they want you to go faster, Aunt Violet,' she said, turning back to face the front. That was not a sentence Clementine had ever thought she would utter. She was usually hanging on for dear life when Aunt Violet was driving. 'I might be late to school if you keep driving like an old granny.'

'I'm being careful, that's all,' Aunt Violet replied. 'And I am no *old granny*, thank you very much! Better late than never, I say.'

Clementine raced into her classroom, where Mr Smee was writing up the day's timetable on the whiteboard.

'Good morning,' he said with a smile. 'Well done on your performance in Basil's documentary. I thought you were terrific.'

Clementine grinned. She saw Poppy and Tilda whispering and went over to see what they were talking about.

'Hello,' Clementine said.

Poppy and Tilda stopped their whispering and looked at her. 'Hi,' the pair giggled.

Clementine's tummy twisted. The girls didn't usually talk behind her back, but now it seemed as though they had a secret. She hoped it wasn't something bad.

Joshua Tribble ran past and poked his tongue out at Clementine. 'Hey flower-girl-movie-star,' he said as he slid onto the carpet in front of Mr Smee's chair.

The teacher gave the lad a warning look before addressing the class. 'Good morning, Year One,' he said, and was greeted with a cheerful reply almost in unison. 'I hope you all had a great weekend. It was wonderful to see so many of you at Penberthy Floss on

Saturday night. I think we should give the star of the show, our very own Clementine Rose Appleby, a huge round of applause for her amazing performance in Mr Hobbs's film.'

The children clapped loudly. Clementine's cheeks went bright red.

'You were really good,' Angus whispered to her.

Clementine could feel herself getting hotter. 'Thanks,' she mumbled.

'It wasn't even a proper movie,' Saskia Baker sneered from the third row. 'It was just on television.'

'Saskia, I'm not enjoying that tone at all.' Mr Smee glared at the girl, who quickly shrank back among the other children. She'd come a long way since the Grandparents' Day Concert but was still prone to vicious outbursts.

Mr Smee started calling the names on the roll, with Clementine first as always. But he kept stopping to look at his watch as if he were waiting for something. The children were getting restless. They usually had the roll marked in less than a minute and were on to their reading groups.

Clementine was wondering why Tilda and Poppy were still giggling as Mr Smee read out Sophie Rousseau's name. She was about to remind the teacher that Sophie was still in Paris when a small voice answered. Clementine quickly turned around and saw Sophie and her mother, Odette, standing in the doorway.

Poppy and Tilda giggled, 'Surprise!'

Clementine leapt to her feet and ran over to her best friend. The two girls hugged and hugged until everyone else in the room faded away. Then they pulled apart and grinned at one another.

'I can't believe you're back,' Clementine said.

Odette's eyes sparkled. 'We could not miss the wedding,' she said.

Clementine launched herself at the woman's middle, giving her a huge hug as well. 'Are you staying?' she asked hopefully.

Sophie nodded. 'Grand-père is much better. He and Madame Joubert are spending lots of time together. She's even been helping him in the shop when she's not putting on little puppet shows in the square.'

'But what about Saskia?' Clementine whispered.

'The Bakers are leaving at the end of the week,' Odette said quietly. 'Mr Baker 'as a new job in the city.'

'Where are you going to stay until they go?' Clementine asked.

'Your house,' Sophie said. 'So Mama can help your mummy with the wedding. Papa is going to make the wedding cake.'

Clementine's heart felt as if it might burst with happiness. Sophie was back for good and Pierre and Odette and Jules too. Clementine couldn't help it and suddenly dissolved into tears.

Odette knelt down. 'What is the matter, *chérie*?'

'My heart is too full and my head is a muddle,' Clementine sobbed.

'Darling girl, it is such a big time for you

and your family.' Odette looked at Mr Smee. 'May I take Clementine outside with Sophie for a few moments? Perhaps we can get a drink of water.'

Roderick Smee nodded. 'Good idea.'

Odette and Sophie held Clementine's hands and the trio walked out into the playground.

Clementine wiped her eyes and tried to stop the tears. 'I must have the wedding wobbles,' she sniffled.

Odette smiled. 'What a lovely way to put it. There is so much anticipation and excitement but lots of change too. You know, I am sure it will be perfect.'

Sophie and Clementine sat down on a bench in the sunshine. 'When we left Paris I cried a lot,' Sophie said. 'Mixed-up tears of happy and sad.'

Clementine squeezed Sophie's hand and smiled. 'Everything feels right again now that you're here.'

And with that the little friends hugged each other tight.

TWO SNOOPS

Violet Appleby arrived home in time to see Mr Johansson walking out the back gate towards the village. She was yet to get a moment alone with the man, but decided there might be another way to find out exactly what he was up to.

She managed to avoid Pertwhistle and Clarissa and headed straight to the Sage Room. It was clear the butler had already been in and made up the bed. Violet walked across to the roll-top bureau and slowly raised the lid. Disappointingly, there was nothing inside except for the Penberthy House Hotel paper and pens that Clarissa supplied to her guests. The old woman tried his suitcase next but found it was locked. She then moved on to the chest of drawers and had just pulled open the first drawer when a floorboard creaked in the hallway.

Aunt Violet eyed the door warily as the handle began to turn. She hastily shut the drawer and cast about for somewhere to hide. Deciding that the wardrobe was the only place she'd fit, she scrambled inside it, holding her breath as light footsteps entered the room.

Violet Appleby's heart was pounding so loudly she thought she'd be discovered any minute now. She heard a drawer open and close, then another. It sounded as though the desk lid was rolled up and then down again. What on earth was the man doing?

Beads of perspiration peppered Violet's brow and she was beginning to feel quite faint.

That was all she needed – to fall down inside the wardrobe with a clatter and a bang.

Violet Appleby wondered just how long she was going to be trapped in the man's wardrobe when the footsteps started heading her way. She pressed her back against the cupboard wall, doing her best to look invisible among the suit coats and trousers. The door opened.

'Oh!' Clarissa gasped, leaping into the air. 'What on earth are you doing in there?'

'Godfathers, Clarissa, what are you trying to do? Kill me?' the old woman demanded.

Clarissa pushed aside the curtain of hangers. 'And I might ask you the same thing,' she said pointedly. 'Why are you snooping about?'

A knock on the door caused both women to jump. 'Ladies,' Digby Pertwhistle said through the door, 'I think our guest might be on his way back.'

Aunt Violet was out of the wardrobe in a flash. Clarissa quickly rearranged the clothes and the pair of them darted out into the hallway.

Digby raised an eyebrow at the women. 'I trust the two of you changed the towels and freshened the flowers.'

Aunt Violet looked as if she was six years old and had just been caught with her hand in the biscuit jar.

The tops of Clarissa's ears turned pink. 'All done,' she squeaked, and the two women scurried away like thieves in the night.

BETTER DAYS

'Mummy, I've had the best day!' Clementine exclaimed as she and Sophie charged up the back steps and into the kitchen.

After her initial surprise, Clementine's day had got better and better. Mr Smee said her story about kissing frogs was her cleverest yet and she got all the answers right on her subtraction sheet. To top it off, her soccer team won the lunchtime derby, with Angus kicking the winning goal.

'That's wonderful, darling,' Clarissa said, pleased to see her daughter was back to her usual happy self. 'And welcome home, Sophie.'

'Where's Aunt Violet?' Clementine asked. 'I want to show her my story, which I got to read to the whole class.'

'It's really funny,' Sophie added, grinning.

Clarissa's heart warmed at the sight of the two friends back together again. 'You'll find her in the study,' she said. 'I'll make you some afternoon tea in the meantime.'

'Thanks, Mummy. Come on, Sophie, let's go,' Clementine said, grabbing her friend's hand and bounding out of the room.

'Ask Aunt Violet if she'd like a cup of tea,' Clarissa called after the pair.

Clementine and Sophie sped along the hall and around the corner to the study, which was located at the back of the house and overlooked the garden. Clementine knocked on the door and poked her head around. Aunt Violet was sitting at her brother's enormous mahogany desk, with her head in her hands, crying. Clementine hesitated.

'What's the matter, Aunt Violet?' she asked, stepping into the room.

The woman raised her head and pulled a tissue from her pocket, wiping her eyes. 'I'm fine, Clementine.'

But that wasn't true at all. When Violet had finally got hold of someone in the solicitor's office who could speak English, she'd been shocked to learn that the letter she'd received was supposed to have been sent six years ago. That meant Eliza had been gone all that while and Violet had never known. She wasn't just a bad mother; she was the worst there ever was.

Sophie hung back in the doorway. She was scared of Aunt Violet at the best of times and seeing her upset wasn't something she'd encountered before.

Clementine eyed the envelope on the desk. It had the same unusual stamps as the one she'd seen in Aunt Violet's handbag the other night. 'Did something in the letter upset you?' she asked, inching forward.

Aunt Violet nodded.

Clementine leant into the old woman and placed her head on her arm. 'Would you like a cup of tea?'

'That would be lovely,' Aunt Violet replied, a small smile on her lips.

'I'll get it,' Sophie offered. She disappeared, leaving Clementine alone with her great-aunt.

'Why are you sad? Don't you want Mummy and Drew to get married?' Clementine asked.

Aunt Violet's eyes widened in surprise. 'Of course I do. Why would you think that?'

'You told Mrs Mogg on Sunday that you thought the house would be too crowded,' Clementine said.

The old woman sniffled into her tissue. 'I wasn't talking about when your mother and Drew got married,' she replied.

'If you are worried about that, I have an idea. You could live in Crabtree Cottage and Will could have your room. Then Mummy will still have the same number of bedrooms for the guests.'

The woman looked crushed. 'I suppose it would only be what I deserve. I was a terrible mother and I'm sure I'm a horrible –'

'I didn't mean it like that,' Clementine said, patting the old woman's shoulder. 'I thought you'd like Crabtree Cottage better because it has two new bathrooms and the tub won't bite your bottom like ours does.'

Aunt Violet laughed. 'So you aren't trying to get rid of me?'

Clementine shook her head. 'I love you and so does everyone else – even Uncle Digby.'

Violet Appleby held out her arms and the girl walked into them. 'I love you too, Clementine,' she whispered.

Digby Pertwhistle arrived with a tray containing a pot of tea, a cup and saucer and a home-made caramel slice, which he set down on the side of the desk. He squeezed the woman's shoulder and, for just a second, she reached up and held on to his hand.

'Aunt Violet isn't moving to Crabtree Cottage,' Clementine said.

Uncle Digby looked at her in surprise.

'Don't ask, Pertwhistle,' Violet said. 'It's far too confusing. Perhaps after I've had my tea you can all help me pull those appalling bows off the front of the house. Honestly, that Sebastian Smote will be the death of me before the end of the week.'

QUESTIONS

The next few days flew by. Clarissa had been careful not to take on too many guests at once and had put a line through Thursday and Friday. Meanwhile, Odette had been doing most of the cooking with Uncle Digby, as Pierre was busy creating a variety of scrumptious treats for the wedding. Mr Smote was a frequent visitor, and on Wednesday morning the marquee was scheduled to go up on the terrace off the billiards room. There were workmen coming and going all over the place and Clementine was having lots of fun talking to each one of them about the wedding. Aunt Violet wasn't so thrilled when she'd discovered three men stringing fairy lights across the back of the house. At least she hadn't cut them down – yet.

On Wednesday afternoon, Clementine found herself wandering the house on her own. Sophie and Jules had accompanied Odette to Highton Mill to have their hair cut, her mother was in the study catching up on paperwork, and Aunt Violet and Uncle Digby were having some sort of mad clear-out upstairs. Clementine stayed out of their way in case they decided she needed to have a special clean-up of her room too. Drew and Will were due for dinner later and Pierre was at the shop, up to his eyeballs in icing sugar and fondant, according to Mr Smote, who had called in to say that the cake was coming along splendidly.

The house was quiet apart from its usual grunts and groans. Clementine sat down on

the main staircase and looked up at the portraits of her ancestors.

'Hello Granny, hello Grandpa,' she said. 'Are you having a good day? I am.'

Clementine babbled away, unaware she had a spectator in the corridor below.

'I wish you could come to the wedding,' she continued. 'But it's probably best you don't. Aunt Violet might get scared and Uncle Digby could have another heart attack. Anyway, it still feels as if you're about, making sure that we're all okay. I know Aunt Violet says mean things about you, Grandpa, but I don't think she really believes them. That's just her.'

The man downstairs was enchanted by the girl's one-sided conversation. He chuckled to himself. 'Are they good listeners?' he asked.

Clementine jumped up and looked over the balustrade. 'Yes, very,' she said, and smiled as soon as she saw who the voice belonged to.

'And do they ever tell you anything?' he asked as he walked upstairs to join her on the landing.

Clementine thought Mr Johansson had such kind eyes. 'Not to worry about things mostly,' she answered truthfully. 'Do you have any children?'

At that moment Aunt Violet and Uncle Digby emerged at the top of the stairs on the floor above. Aunt Violet was about to speak when the butler put a finger to his lips.

'Shhh, she's probably chatting to her grandparents,' he whispered.

Aunt Violet rolled her eyes then grinned, but she wasn't expecting a man's voice to speak next.

'I have a little girl,' Mr Johansson said to Clementine, 'but I haven't seen her in a long, long time.'

'What's he doing talking to Clemmie again?' Violet huffed. 'I thought he'd be gone by now.'

'Does she live far away from you?' asked Clementine.

'Yes, I'm afraid so,' Mr Johansson answered.

'I'm sure you'll see her again one day soon,' Clementine said. 'You know, you only have to think of her and she'll feel you in her heart.'

Aunt Violet's eyes filled with tears. Uncle Digby put his arm around the woman and she turned into his chest.

'You are very wise for such a young girl,' Mr Johansson said. 'How do you know such things?'

'When Sophie moved to Paris, I missed her so much that sometimes it made me cry. When I got upset Mummy would tell me to close my eyes and think about her and I would feel her right here,' Clementine said, crossing her hands over her heart.

Aunt Violet couldn't stand it a moment longer. She burst into racking sobs and was quickly rushed away by Uncle Digby. Clementine looked up just in time to see them disappearing and wondered what the matter was now.

'Are you going home today?' she asked, turning back to Mr Johansson.

The man shook his head. 'Not home, but I am leaving to make some special arrangements in the city. I think I will be back again,' he said. 'Very soon.'

'You must really like it here to stay for so many days,' Clementine observed. 'What was the best thing? Mummy says it's helpful to know what guests enjoy the most so she can work on the other things that aren't so good.'

'Oh, there were *many* things. Delicious breakfasts, a comfy bed, a hot shower,' the man said. 'A lovely little girl to meet.'

'Thank you,' Clementine said. 'And no offence, Mr Johansson, but that fish paste smelled really bad.'

'It is an acquired taste, my dear,' the man replied, his eyes twinkling. He took the girl's hand in his. 'Farewell for now, Clementine Rose Appleby. I will make sure we meet again soon.'

'Goodbye, Mr Johansson.' Clementine smiled and gave him a wave. He was definitely one of her favourite guests in a very long time.

SNIP!

The excitement at Penberthy House was building. By Friday afternoon Sebastian Smote and his team had finished decorating the marquee. The ceiling was swathed in white silk and bunting, peppered with the prettiest blue and pink flowers crisscrossed from one side to the other all the way along. The painted timber chairs were exactly the same colour as Clementine's dress and there were more fairy lights than stars in the sky. Clementine thought it was the most beautiful tent Mr Smote had ever created and that was without the flowers that were being delivered first thing Saturday morning. Aunt Violet had insisted that she would do the arrangements and had enlisted Ana Hobbs and Odette to help her.

On the morning of the wedding, Clementine awoke with a stomach full of butterflies.

'Today is the big day,' she whispered to Lavender, and jumped out of bed to give the little pig a scratch between her ears.

Clementine was about to pull on her dressing-gown when she spotted the white bag hanging from the front of the wardrobe door. Unable to resist taking a quick peek at her flower girl's dress, Clementine unzipped the covering. She marvelled at the delicate embroidered flowers that Mrs Mogg had added. As her eyes swept over the fabric, Clementine noticed a tiny loose thread.

'That shouldn't be there,' she said to herself.

Having watched Mrs Mogg work on countless garments, Clementine knew just what to do.

She fetched a pair of scissors from her pencil case and gave the pesky thread a snip. To her shock, three pink flowers fell instantly into the palm of her hand.

'Oh no!' Clementine gasped.

There was now a large gaping hole in the middle of her dress. Her cheeks burned as she thought about how upset her mother and Mrs Mogg would be when they found out. Aunt Violet would be furious! Clementine felt awful and was convinced she had ruined the whole wedding.

Gulping down sobs, she carefully laid the dress on her bed and tried very hard to think of how she could fix it. The problem was, she'd never sewn anything in her life. And then she saw the answer sitting on her desk. What better way to make sure the flowers didn't fall off again but by using a stapler?

She picked up the contraption and swallowed hard. Clementine held a flower in one hand and the stapler in the other and was just about to give it a go when Sophie pushed open the door.

'Guess what, Clemmie? Basil phoned to say Cosmo is missing. We're going to – *Oh la vache!* What are you doing?' she exclaimed, clutching her cheeks in horror.

Clementine's chin trembled. 'My dress is broken,' she said.

'You can't fix it like that.' Sophie's eyes were huge. 'I'll get Mama.'

Before Clementine had time to object, Sophie dashed away and returned with Odette in tow. The woman had brought her small sewing box and flashed Clementine a reassuring smile.

'It looks like I got 'ere in the nick of time, *chérie*,' she said, and set to work mending Clementine's dress.

Meanwhile, downstairs, Aunt Violet was pacing the length of the kitchen.

'They were supposed to be here by now,' she grouched, staring daggers at the clock on the wall.

'Why don't you give the flower farm a call?' Uncle Digby suggested.

Violet Appleby strode over to the telephone and dialled the number, which rang and rang until it stopped. 'Good grief, where are they?' she blustered. 'If the flowers don't arrive soon, we'll never get the arrangements done in time.'

Digby put the kettle on, having decided that the best way to calm the situation was tea – and lots of it.

'Hello, hello, who's getting married today?' Sebastian Smote's voice trilled through the hallway, heralding his arrival.

Aunt Violet looked up and gasped, shielding her eyes. The man had worn some ridiculous outfits before but this one took the biscuit. Her lips quivered with distaste. 'What on earth are you wearing?' she asked.

The man struck a pose. 'Isn't it divine? I wanted to be perfect for Clarissa's wedding.'

But neither divine nor perfect were the words on the tip of Violet Appleby's tongue.

She wasn't sure when puce-coloured three-piece suits, spotted blue cravats and matching pocket squares adorned with more jewellery than she'd ever owned had come into vogue. There was one thing for sure – no one was going to miss him this afternoon. To top off his crime against fashion, the man wore a fedora at a most unsuitable jaunty angle.

'You look ridiculous,' Aunt Violet said, unwilling to hold her tongue a second longer. 'You should change at once and, while you're at it, you can get rid of that dreadful cherub fountain in the middle of the front lawn. It's not staying. And where are my flowers?'

For a second Mr Smote looked positively stung. He recovered quickly, having been on the receiving end of the woman's barbs many times before. Besides, he knew she didn't mean it. If there was one thing the two of them had in common, it was an extraordinary sense of style.

'Surprise, surprise, I have a matching fountain for the back lawn too,' Sebastian mumbled, then consulted his pocket watch.

Violet glared at the man. 'What did you say?'

'Nothing at all and yes, you're right. The flowers should have well and truly arrived by now,' he said, frowning.

'Then *do* something. You're in charge of the wedding. Make it happen!' Violet ordered.

Sebastian pulled out his telephone and dialled, running into the exact same problem that Violet had encountered minutes before.

She looked at him expectantly. 'Well?'

Mr Smote's lip curled. 'This is most unlike my supplier. Mrs Trelawning is very reliable. Unless you gave her the wrong time when you changed the order the other day?'

'I did no such thing!' Aunt Violet grabbed her handbag from the dresser. 'If your beloved Mrs Trelawning can't deliver on her promises, I guess I'll have to collect the flowers myself.'

She stormed into the foyer, past Clementine and Sophie, who were thudding down the stairs. Jules had taken himself out into the garden to search for Cosmo when his sister had gone to find Clementine.

'Where are you going, Aunt Violet?' Clementine asked, running after her.

'To get the flowers,' the woman called, rushing out to her car in front of the garage and pulling open the driver's door. She fished about in her handbag for the keys then realised she'd left them inside. 'Drat,' she griped and charged back into the house.

'We should help her,' Clementine said. In truth, she wanted to be as far away from her dress as possible, lest she wreak more havoc upon it. 'And we can keep an eye out for Cosmo on the way.'

Clementine and Sophie climbed into the shiny red car and buckled their seatbelts.

Aunt Violet raced out the door and jumped into the driver's seat, spinning her wheels on the gravel and roaring off down the road.

Clementine and Sophie looked at each other and giggled, but Aunt Violet didn't hear a thing. She was a woman on a mission. It wasn't until she'd overtaken three other cars that Clementine finally piped up.

'Aunt Violet, I thought you weren't going to speed anymore,' she said from the back seat.

Startled, the old woman swerved and almost lost control of the vehicle altogether. She quickly regained her composure and planted her foot on the brake, bringing the car to a screeching halt.

'What are you two doing in here?' she sputtered, clutching at her chest.

Clementine looked back at her great-aunt with wide, innocent eyes. 'Helping,' she replied.

Violet huffed loudly. 'I wouldn't be so sure of that.'

To prove her usefulness, Clementine suggested they take a short cut to the flower farm. 'It's down that road up there,' she said, and leaned forward between the seats, pointing.

Aunt Violet looked at her dubiously. 'Are you absolutely positive?'

'Yes, that's the way Mummy and I went with Mr Smote a few weeks ago,' the child replied. Sophie nodded in support.

Violet Appleby shrugged. 'Very well, then,' she said. 'What's the worst that could happen?'

She turned left into the road, just as the van loaded with her delivery puttered past in the opposite direction.

It was a pity no one in the car noticed.

STUCK

Violet Appleby drove on past fields of colourful blooms.

'Surely it can't be much further,' she muttered, hunched over the steering wheel.

Clementine looked out the window, trying to remember. She had a bad feeling that the road they were searching for had been the next one along and not this one at all.

Suddenly, a frisky black cow dashed across in front of them, only metres ahead.

'Look out!' Clementine yelled.

The old woman swerved sharply to miss the beast. The car skidded off the side of the road and into a muddy ditch, jolting to a halt.

Aunt Violet looked around at the girls. 'Is everyone all right?' she asked.

Clementine and Sophie nodded.

'It's lucky you were driving slowly for a change,' Clementine said.

'Where on earth did that animal come from?' Aunt Violet shook her head and smoothed her hair. She put the gears into reverse and stamped her foot on the accelerator. There was no time to lose.

But the car didn't move.

Sophie and Clementine turned and looked behind them as a shower of thick brown mud spattered all over the boot and onto the rear windscreen.

'We're bogged,' Clementine said.

'But I don't have time to be bogged,' Aunt Violet snapped. 'We have got to collect the flowers and get back.'

'This is a disaster,' Clementine whispered to Sophie. 'We're going to have to walk home and it's really far. What if we miss the wedding?'

Aunt Violet persisted with her foot on the accelerator until the girls could no longer see out of the back window. With an exasperated grunt, the old woman stepped out of the car, promptly disappearing up to her waist in the oozy muck.

Clementine and Sophie gasped.

'Help!' Aunt Violet yelped.

The girls hastily unbuckled their seatbelts and peered out at the muddy quagmire. Sophie slid back to her side and opened the door.

'Clemmie, this way!' she urged.

The two girls exited the car from the other side and ran around to see what they could do.

Aunt Violet was clinging to the open car door, doing her utmost to stay upright.

'Argh!' the woman squawked, struggling to lift her leg.

'You're going to have to get into the car and climb across the seats,' Clementine said.

'But what about my upholstery?' the woman moaned. 'It's cream.'

Clementine shrugged. 'You could wade out around the back. It doesn't look as deep there.'

Aunt Violet wiped her forehead, leaving a long brown streak.

Just as she was about to try her luck, Basil's car appeared over the rise. Clementine and Sophie jumped up and down, waving their arms to get the man's attention. Basil pulled up in the middle of the road and he and his three children leapt out of the car.

'What a relief that you came along!' Clementine exclaimed. 'Aunt Violet is stuck.'

'Help!' the woman yelled. 'Get me out of here.'

Basil ran around to the driver's side of the car and found a dry piece of ground to stand on. He couldn't help himself and laughed loudly. 'Oh, Miss Appleby, are you all right?'

'Do I look as if I'm all right? Don't just stand there! Do something!' Aunt Violet ordered.

'Here, Dad.' Teddy jogged further along the road and located a long branch. He dragged it back to his father, and the two of them and Mintie held on to it while Aunt Violet hauled herself out of the bog.

'Look at me!' the woman wailed.

Basil smiled, hoping he had a towel or two in his car so she could wipe off some of the thick goo before she got in. 'It's nothing a shower won't fix,' he said amiably, 'and think how smooth your skin will be. Some women pay a fortune for a good old mud bath.'

Back at Penberthy House, Jules had combed the garden for Cosmo and was completely baffled about where the girls had disappeared to. A van had arrived a little while ago and Mr Smote had been rushing around directing the delivery of buckets upon buckets of flowers. Jules decided to head up to see if the girls were in Clementine's bedroom. As he ascended the main staircase, Clarissa poked her head out of the Rose Room, where she was getting ready. She looked like a flower herself, with huge rollers covering her head.

'Jules, have you seen Clemmie?' she asked.

The lad shook his head. 'I'm just looking for her and Sophie,' he replied.

Clarissa smiled. 'Well, when you find them, can you tell Clemmie that she needs to come and get her hair done?'

Jules grinned and nodded.

'I know – I hope I look better than this once they're finished too,' Clarissa giggled.

Jules raced to the top floor and poked his head into Clementine's room. The girls weren't there. He walked along the hall to the end of the corridor and into the bedroom at the rear of the house, which overlooked the garden. He could see a lot from there.

As he scanned the grounds he spotted something moving at the western edge of the marquee. It looked like a tail swishing back and forth and it didn't belong to Lavender or Pharaoh.

'Cosmo!' the boy gasped. He lifted the windowpane and called to the cavoodle.

Sebastian Smote heard the lad's cry as he was carrying two vases full of flowers from the kitchen. 'What's going on up there?' he yelled.

'Cosmo, the Hobbs's dog,' Jules shouted, pointing at the creature. But the man didn't appear to understand.

Jules shut the window and bolted to the back stairs, taking two or three at a time.

Outside, Cosmo had found something to play with. He was tugging and tugging and growling and shaking his head, trying to get the knot free when, with one last pull, a row of bunting fell to the ground. Delighted with his handiwork, Cosmo grabbed the end of it in his teeth. He ran with the length of material and its triangular flaps trailing behind.

Sebastian Smote was stepping into the marquee when he was almost bowled over by the beast and his prize. 'What are you doing, you naughty dog?'

The man spun around twice and barely managed to keep hold of the vases in his arms. But Cosmo was having way too much fun. He wanted the man to join in, so he ran around and around in circles until Sebastian's legs were tangled. Jules ran over and caught one of the vases before it hit the ground. Then he scooped up the pup and held him tight.

'Good heavens, where did this canine intruder come from?' Sebastian steadied himself and began to unwrap the length of material from around his legs.

'He belongs to the Hobbses,' Jules said. 'Don't worry, I'll look after him.'

'What a mess!' Sebastian wailed, and began directing his helpers to put things back together. In tearing down the bunting, Cosmo had also managed to knock over several chairs, a table and the second cherub fountain Sebastian had snuck in at the last minute.

Jules carried Cosmo around to the front of the house just as Basil pulled up in the driveway.

'Cosmo!' the children squealed, tumbling out of the car.

'Where did you two go?' Jules asked Clementine and Sophie. His eyes almost popped out of his head when he spotted Aunt Violet covered from top to bottom in a crusty layer of mud.

'Aunt Violet ran off the road and we went in a bog,' Clementine explained.

'It was hardly my fault,' the woman grumbled, and stormed into the house.

Basil took Cosmo from Jules's arms and cuddled the dog. 'I hope he didn't get up to any mischief.'

Jules shrugged. 'Only a little. Clemmie, you need to go upstairs to the Rose Room and have your hair done.' The boy was glad he remembered.

'Sophie, can you make sure Lavender is wearing her ribbon and can you bring her out for the ceremony?' Clementine asked her friend. They'd arranged it all before and Odette had offered to help tie the bow.

Ana and Odette appeared on the front steps. 'Do you need a hand with anything?' Basil asked.

'We're all done.' Ana smiled. 'But we'd better hurry home and get ready. Drew called to say he'd left his bow tie here, so we've got to drop it off to him at Crabtree Cottage.'

'Come on, Jules and Sophie,' Odette called. 'Time to get changed.'

Aunt Violet charged through the house and out to the marquee, where Sebastian Smote and his team were putting the finishing touches to the flowers. He looked at her, his lips quivering.

'Don't say a word,' she ordered, inspecting the arrangements.

The man gulped, waiting for her to deliver her judgement.

'They'll do,' she said, and stomped away inside.

FAMILY MATTERS

Clementine raced upstairs to the Rose Room.

'Sorry I'm late, Mummy. We got stuck in a bog with Aunt Violet but we're back now, except her car is still in the mud,' she explained. Her mother was sitting at the dressing table and there was a tall lady with long red fingernails doing her hair. Another woman was dusting her face with powder.

'I don't think I want to know the details, Clemmie,' Clarissa said, and spun around. 'As long as everyone is safe.'

'Look at you, Mummy,' the child gasped. 'You're a princess.'

Clarissa smiled. 'I think Bella and Teresa have performed nothing short of a miracle.'

'Your turn, Clemmie,' Bella said.

Clarissa stood up and Clementine jumped into the chair.

'Teresa, would you mind helping me into my dress?' Clarissa asked.

Clementine noticed that her mother's gown was hanging in a long white bag on the front of the wardrobe and hers was hanging next to it.

'No peeking, Clemmie,' Clarissa reminded her, then went to the other side of the room to get dressed.

Clementine marvelled at the way Bella swept up her hair and had it looking absolutely flawless in no time. Finally, the woman positioned the little blue headpiece of flowers on her head. Teresa then gave Clementine a light dusting of blusher on her cheeks, some mascara and a smidge of pale pink lip gloss.

Clementine closed her eyes. 'Are you ready, Mummy?' she asked.

'Yes,' Clarissa said.

Clementine glanced over at her mother in her lacy gown. It had long sleeves and a tiny waistline, with a silk skirt that cascaded to the floor. Clementine had never seen anyone look so beautiful.

'I don't even have enough words in my brain to tell you how perfect you are, Mummy,' Clementine said.

Clarissa smiled. 'Thank you. You are a funny one, my darling.'

Teresa helped Clementine into her dress and shoes, and Bella sprayed Clarissa's hair.

'That's Granny's tiara,' Clementine said, realising that her mother's hairpiece was an important family heirloom.

'Well, why not?' Clarissa said. 'You only get married once.'

'Unless you're Aunt Violet,' Clementine giggled.

There was a knock on the door and Uncle Digby poked his head around.

'Heavens, look at my girls.' He wiped a tear from his eye, then nodded at Bella and Teresa. 'Would you two clever ladies like a cup of tea downstairs? The bride has a visitor.'

'Who is it?' Clarissa asked. She couldn't imagine what could be so urgent that they needed to see her on her wedding day.

'It's Mr Johansson,' Uncle Digby said, stepping back to let the man into the room.

Clementine broke into a smile. 'Hello there. I know you said you were coming back, but today's probably not the best day. Mummy's getting married in a little while and we don't have any rooms for you to stay in.'

He smiled at Clementine. 'I won't be staying. My timing is terrible, but you must know why I came, Lady Appleby.'

Clarissa stood in the open doorway and wrapped her arm protectively around her daughter. 'Please don't take her away from me,' she whispered.

Clementine looked at her mother, then at Mr Johansson, her blue eyes widening in confusion.

'Oh, Lady Appleby, I am so sorry. That was never my intention,' the man said.

Clarissa looked up. 'But you're her father, aren't you?'

He shook his head. 'No, but I have been looking for this little girl for a long time.'

'Who are you?' Clementine stared at the man. She'd never really thought a lot about her father before and was all of a sudden feeling very mixed up.

'I am your father's brother. He passed away in an accident just before you were born. Then your mother, Eliza, disappeared and we never knew what happened to you. When I learned about her illness, I searched and searched and it has taken me all these years. She left you in a very good place.

'I wanted to find you. Not only because you are my niece, but your father has left you a trust. There is enough money to pay for your education and perhaps even buy a house when you are older.' The man reached inside his coat pocket and passed a photograph to Clarissa. 'This is Theodore.'

Clementine looked at her mother. 'Like the warthog.'

'You did make me smile when you told me your warthog's name was Theodore,' Mr Johansson said, 'but I can assure you your father was nothing like him. He was clever and funny and smart just like you. And he would have been so very proud.'

Clarissa handed Clementine the picture.

The tiny girl studied it for quite some time before she spoke. 'Is that really my daddy?' she asked. 'He looks kind. I'm sorry he's not here anymore.'

'I am sorry too,' Stefan Johansson said. 'But life is full of twists and turns and you have found the best place in the world to be.'

'That's true,' Clementine said. 'And now I have another uncle as well as Uncle Digby, and in a little while I'm getting a new daddy and a brother too. My family has got really big today.'

'I am sorry, Lady Appleby. I had to know for sure that I had the right child. I have spent the past week getting the papers in order,' Stefan said, 'and tonight I must return home.'

The woman smiled at him. 'Perhaps you should call me Clarissa. We are family, after all. Now, you must stay for the wedding. Speaking of which, we should get going or Drew will think I've stood him up.'

Mr Johansson grinned. 'Of course. I'll see you downstairs.'

Clementine held out the photograph to give back to him.

'Oh no, it is yours to keep,' he said with a smile.

'Thank you,' Clementine said, and hurried over to place it carefully on the dressing table before returning to her mother's side.

Digby Pertwhistle arrived back in the doorway. 'Is everything all right?' he asked Clarissa.

'Yes,' she said, wiping away a stray tear.

'I have another uncle,' Clementine informed the old butler.

'I thought you might.' Uncle Digby smiled at the child. He looked at Clarissa. 'Ready, my dear?'

Clarissa beamed and took his arm. 'Ready as I'll ever be.'

Clementine fixed the bottom of her mother's dress and passed her an exquisite bouquet of pink and white peonies. Then she picked up her basket of petals and they descended the stairs to make the short walk to the garden, where Drew and Will and all their friends and family were waiting.

GRANNY

'Congratulations, my darlings.' Aunt Violet kissed the newlyweds as they entered the marquee, following the lawn ceremony.

'Thank you, Aunt Violet,' Clarissa said. 'We couldn't have done it without you, and the flowers are magnificent.'

Sebastian Smote was hovering nearby with a smug smile on his face.

Clementine and her family took their places at the head table, which sat on a podium overlooking the party. Uncle Digby was on the end next to Aunt Violet, then came Clementine, her mother, Drew and Will. All their friends were there and even Mrs Bottomley had wangled herself an invitation. Sophie was keeping an eye on Lavender, who looked adorable in her big pink bow. Everyone had laughed as she'd snuffled down the aisle behind Clementine, hoovering up the rose petals the child had sprinkled. Fortunately, Will didn't drop the rings, so Lavender didn't get a chance to eat them too.

Violet Appleby looked across the room and caught sight of Mr Johansson sitting with Ethel. 'Godfathers! What's he doing here?'

'He's my new uncle,' Clementine said, as if it were the most obvious thing in the world.

Violet recoiled in horror.

'I'll tell you all about it later,' Uncle Digby whispered to the woman, 'but there's no cause for alarm.'

Luckily, there were food and speeches to distract Aunt Violet for the moment.

The wedding feast was spectacular with beef tenderloins and potato au gratin, crispy beans and honeyed carrots. Clementine was starving and ate all of her lunch. Following their main course, Drew stood up and made a speech, which saw more than a few of the guests bringing out their tissues. But it was not long after when he nodded at Mr Smote and the marquee was plunged into darkness that there wasn't a dry eye in the place.

'Clarissa, I must confess that the project I've been working on lately wasn't really work at all,' he said. A projector light beamed a series of photographs and moving images on to the ceiling of the marquee, accompanied by a soundtrack of music they both loved. What followed was the most amazing record of their relationship, from the first day that Drew had arrived with Basil at Penberthy House to shoot the documentary.

Clarissa stood up and spoke beautifully about her new husband, although she warned that their dancing might not be as good as she'd hoped due to a lack of practice.

Clementine was up next with her wedding poem called 'What is Love?'. By the time she reached the end, Aunt Violet was sniffling into her tissue with her head resting on Uncle Digby's shoulder. Even Ethel Bottomley was wiping away tears. Mr Mogg stood up and led all the guests in a standing ovation and Clementine took a bow. Uncle Digby delivered his speech after that and made everyone laugh and smile.

The happy couple then cut Pierre's magnificent wedding cake before proceeding to the dance floor, where they stunned the crowd with their perfect waltz. Clarissa twirled and swayed in her husband's arms, savouring every second of their wonderful day. Clementine and Will giggled when Uncle Digby took Aunt Violet by the hand and the pair started shimmying and shaking like teenagers. Soon the dance floor was packed, and Clementine and Will joined the throng.

Clementine spotted Sophie dancing with Poppy but couldn't see Lavender. She thought

the tiny pig must be asleep under one of the tables. After all, it had been an exhausting day and Lavender loved to nap.

Over in one corner of the marquee, Mr Smote was surveying the happy crowd, his hips swaying to the beat, when Clementine noticed one of the waiter's whisper something to him. Sebastian's face turned bright red.

'Wait until I get my hands on that pig,' the man fumed. 'She will be pork roast for Christmas dinner!'

Clementine scanned the marquee for any sign of her pet. 'Uh-oh, I have to go,' she said, leaving Will in the middle of the dance floor.

Aunt Violet caught wind that something was amiss and dumped Digby to investigate. Seeing Smote in a tizzy almost always spelled disaster in her experience. 'What's going on?' she demanded.

'The desserts are ruined and my reputation along with it!' Sebastian exclaimed as he scurried through the billiard room towards the kitchen. 'It was that greedy, porky pig!'

'Lavender!' Aunt Violet exhaled.

'Lavender doesn't even like dessert, Aunt Violet,' Clementine said, running alongside the pair. 'But Pharaoh does – he ate the cake at the pet day. Remember?'

'My boy wouldn't do anything as ghastly as that,' the old woman huffed. 'He's a perfect puss.'

Clementine raced ahead with Aunt Violet in her peacock-blue suit charging after her.

Mr Smote clutched his hands to head. 'Pierre will be devastated. That poor man has worked for days, slaving over hot stoves and blazing ovens.'

Clementine ran through the swinging door into the kitchen and skidded to a halt.

She gasped.

Aunt Violet gasped.

Mr Smote threw his hands into the air and burst into tears.

Pierre's beautiful desserts were smooshed all over the floor.

'Lavender!' Clementine called out.

She poked her head into the butler's pantry, but it wasn't Lavender she found. Curled up on the bottom shelf was Pharaoh. Aunt Violet and Sebastian Smote followed the child into the room.

Clementine turned to face the pair. 'I told you so.'

Sebastian ran his index finger along Pharaoh's face, accumulating a fat glob of cream as he did. He stuck his finger into his mouth. 'It seems Clementine was right. That was our dessert.'

'That was really disgusting,' Clementine said, wrinkling her nose. 'You shouldn't eat food off a cat's face.'

'Oh no,' Aunt Violet sighed. 'What will we do? It's all my fault. Pharaoh, I thought I trained you better than that.'

Sebastian stuck his nose into the air. 'It's a disaster. The worst disaster I have ever had at any wedding and I have looked after lots of weddings.'

A waiter poked his head into the room. 'Excuse me, Mr Smote. The desserts are served.'

'What? But they are ruined,' Sebastian said, cradling his face in his manicured hands.

'Those were the leftovers,' the young man said sheepishly.

Sebastian rushed at the startled fellow and hugged him tightly. 'Oh, darling angel! That's the best news I've heard all day.'

'Thank heavens for that,' Violet said. 'Come along, Clemmie. We don't want to miss out.'

Clementine took the woman's hand and they walked back through the house.

As they reached the entrance foyer at the bottom of the stairs, Aunt Violet suddenly remembered something. 'Clementine, what did you mean before when you said that Mr Johansson was your new uncle?'

'His brother was my daddy,' Clementine said. 'He died before I was born.'

Aunt Violet gasped, her eyes filling with tears.

'It's all right, Granny. I know there wasn't just one tragedy, there were two,' Clementine said.

Aunt Violet looked up at the portrait of her sister-in-law.

Clementine shook her head and stared at her great-aunt. 'I was talking to you, Aunt Violet.'

The woman gulped. 'But how? When did you find out?' she said, her voice barely a whisper.

'I worked it out quite a while ago, when Mummy told me about Eliza. But you never wanted to be old and you always said that grannies were old people, so I thought it was better that you didn't know,' Clementine said. 'Eliza was my mother, but she got sick. She gave me to Mummy so I wouldn't be on my own and Mummy wouldn't be either.'

Violet's lip trembled and tears spilled onto her cheeks. 'Well, I'm not old, am I?' she said, finding some strength in her voice. 'I can be a young granny. And I am very happy to be *your* granny for the rest of my days.'

Clementine looked at Aunt Violet and, for the second time that week, she felt as if her heart might just burst with happiness.

What is Love?

by Clementine Rose Appleby

Love is
a chat with Granny and Grandpa
and a treat from Mrs Mogg.
It's games with Tilda and Teddy
and Cosmo, their naughty dog.

It's Uncle Digby's breakfasts,
it's Lavender tickling my cheeks.
It's building cubbies with Sophie and Jules,
and Pharaoh snuggles when I'm asleep.

It's adventures with Aunt Violet,
who drives way too fast,
but I love her funny stories
and at least we never come last.

It's hugs and kisses from Mummy –
I'll never be too big for those.
It's my new brother, Will, and father, Drew,
who I'm so glad Mummy chose.

CAST OF CHARACTERS

The Appleby household

Clementine Rose Appleby	Six-year-old daughter of Lady Clarissa
Lavender	Clemmie's teacup pig
Lady Clarissa Appleby	Clementine's mother and the owner of Penberthy House
Digby Pertwhistle	Butler at Penberthy House
Aunt Violet Appleby	Clementine's grandfather's sister

Pharaoh	Aunt Violet's beloved sphynx cat
Drew Barnsley	Clarissa's husband
Will Barnsley	Drew's son and Clementine's stepbrother

School staff and students

Mrs Ethel Bottomley	Teacher at Ellery Prep
Mr Roderick Smee	Year One teacher
Sophie Rousseau	Clementine's best friend
Poppy Bauer	Clementine's good friend
Araminta Hobbs	Eleven-year-old daughter of Basil and Ana
Tilda Hobbs	Twin sister of Teddy, classmate
Teddy Hobbs	Twin brother of Tilda, classmate
Angus Archibald	Friend in Clementine's class
Joshua Tribble	Clementine's classmate
Saskia Baker	Clementine's classmate

Friends and village folk

Margaret Mogg	Owner of Penberthy Floss village shop
Claws Mogg	Margaret's tabby cat
Basil Hobbs	Documentary filmmaker and neighbour
Ana Hobbs (nee Barkov)	Former prima ballerina and neighbour
Cosmo	The Hobbs's cavoodle pup
Father Bob	Village minister
Adrian	Father Bob's dribbly bulldog
Pierre Rousseau	Owner of Pierre's Patisserie in Highton Mill
Odette Rousseau	Sophie's mother
Jules Rousseau	Eight-year-old brother of Sophie
Mrs Tribble	Joshua's mother

Others

Sebastian Smote	Wedding planner

Mr Johansson,	Guests at Penberthy
Mr and Mrs Swizzle	House
Bella	Hairdresser
Teresa	Make-up artist

ABOUT
THE AUTHOR

Jacqueline Harvey taught for many years in girls' boarding schools. She is the author of the bestselling Alice-Miranda series and the Clementine Rose series, and was awarded Honour Book in the 2006 Australian CBC Awards for her picture book *The Sound of the Sea*. She now writes full-time and is working on more Alice-Miranda and Clementine Rose adventures.

www.jacquelineharvey.com.au

JACQUELINE
SUPPORTS

Jacqueline Harvey is a passionate educator who enjoys sharing her love of reading and writing with children and adults alike. She is an ambassador for Dymocks Children's Charities and Room to Read. Find out more at www.dcc.gofundraise.com.au and www.roomtoread.org.

Puzzles, quizzes and yummy things to cook!

THE CLEMENTINE ROSE

Busy Day Book

Out now

LIV
April 2018